The Spookster's Handbook

Peter Eldin

With Drawings by Roger Smith

Sterling Publishing Co., Inc.   New York

Allen County Public Library
Ft. Wayne, Indiana

Library of Congress Cataloging-in-Publication Data

Eldin, Peter.
   The spookster's handbook / by Peter Eldin ; drawings by Roger
Smith.
      p.   cm.
   Includes index.
   Summary: More than fifty fiendishly funny tricks and monstrous
mischief to entertain your friends, with humorous drawings, riddles,
and trivia.
   ISBN 0-8069-5742-5
   1. Wit and humor, Juvenile. 2. Practical jokes. 3. American wit
and humor, Pictorial.   [1. Tricks. 2. Practical jokes. 3. Wit and
humor.] I. Smith, Roger, 1930–   ill. II. Title.
PN6163.E44   1989
793.5--dc20   89-32659
                                                        CIP
                                                          AC

Published in 1989 by Sterling Publishing Co., Inc.
387 Park Avenue South, New York, New York 10016
The material in this book was compiled and adapted
from *The Spookster's Handbook*, published in
the United Kingdom by Armada, Collins Publishing Group, London
© Eldin Editorial Services 1984
Distributed in Canada by Sterling Publishing
% Canadian Manda Group, P.O. Box 920, Station U
Toronto, Ontario, Canada M8Z 5P9
Manufactured in the United States of America
All rights reserved
Sterling ISBN 0-8069-5743-3 (pbk.)

CONTENTS

By the Same Author

Amazing Ghosts & Other Mysteries
Amazing Pranks & Blunders
The Trickster's Handbook

1
MAKING MONSTERS

The Bug-Eyed Monster

Have you ever seen a bug-eyed monster? If you have—or even if you haven't—here's a good way to make yourself into one.

All you need is a Ping-Pong ball and a piece of elastic. Carefully cut the ball in half and make a hole at opposite sides of each half. Tie the elastic carefully to the balls, as shown in the illustration. Make sure the elastic is long enough to fit around your head comfortably.

Now use a ballpoint or felt-tipped pen to draw a pupil (an eye, that is) on the front of each half ball. If you want to look especially horrible, use a repulsive color, like slime green. But if you want to look peculiar, paint each eye a different color (bloodshot red for one, maybe, and yucky-yellow for the other). Push a pin through the center of each half-ball-pupil so that you'll be able to see through them.

Place the contraption around your head with the Ping-Pong balls over your eyes. You'll look extremely strange—even stranger than you do normally.

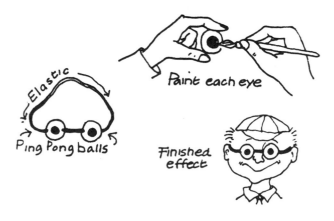

Elastic

Ping Pong balls

Paint each eye

Finished effect

The Mutant Bug

Tie a knot into each corner of a handkerchief or paper napkin. Secretly place a lemon under it. Then show it to your friends.

If you prod the "bug" with your finger, it will move across the table in a very peculiar way. Another method for making the bug move: Place it on a tray and then tilt the tray slightly.

To make the bug even weirder, you could draw or paint some eyes on it.

How to Look Absolutely Revolting

This is a very simple way to look absolutely revolting. If you look absolutely revolting already, you don't need to read any further. But if you're fantastically good-looking (like the author of this book), then read on.

You need a chunk of orange peel (take the fruit off it first). About a quarter of the whole peel is right. Cut a slit along the center, as shown in the first picture. Now make a bunch of short slits across the first slit (as shown in the second picture).

If you now push the skin out from the center and slip the peel into the front of your mouth, you will look like Dracula on a bad day.

If you want to make yourself look even more monstrous, cut out one or two of the "teeth," or blacken them with a black felt-tipped pen.

Wear these false teeth when you visit the dentist, and you could give him the shock of his life.

Warty Witch

Look at most old pictures of witches and you'll see that they are covered with warts (the witches, not the pictures). Here is an easy way to make your own warts, if you want to look like a witch.

All you need is a piece of bread. Take a small pellet of bread about the size of a pea and roll it between your fingers. If you now wet it, you'll find it will stick to your face and make you look very witchy.

Put several of them on your face and you really will be ugly.

If the pellet won't stick properly, mix a paste from flour and water and use it to glue the wart in place.

The Remarkable Living Head

With the help of a friend you can create a horrible bearded monster with no body! It helps if your friend is a horrible bearded monster to start with. But if he—or she—is not, then you can do it this way:

Get your friend to lie on his back under a table. He must throw his head back as far as possible so that the top of his head is on the floor and his chin is pointing straight up towards the edge of the table.

Place a hat on your friend's chin so that it comes close to covering his nostrils.

Use a felt-tipped pen—or an old lipstick—to draw a mouth on your friend's forehead. You can use the same lipstick or other makeup to draw in a weird-looking nose and lines around the eyes.

Now put a tablecloth on the table and let it hang down until it reaches the floor. Position the cloth around your friend's head, so that only his head is visible.

There is no point in creating this strange monster if no one is around to see it. So the next step is to invite your family and friends to see the Remarkable Living Head.

If anyone wants to know where this amazing creature came from, you can say, "He was a man who had lots of problems. They mounted up day-by-day and he didn't know what to do. One day, the police knocked at his door. He panicked and lost his head."

Well, you get the idea. . . .

Skeleton of a Leaf

Making skeleton leaves used to be popular during the last century, but it isn't done very often now. You can use the leaves from many different kinds of trees, but the best are lime, apple, maple, poplar and pear. Pick them while the leaves are still in good condition and fairly young, and only choose ones that are healthy-looking and free of spots.

Place all the leaves together in a jar of clean rainwater. Put the jar in a warm place for about a month, so that the leaves have time to decompose. The leaves may smell a little at this stage—due to the rotting leaf tissue—but the smell will soon disappear.

Put one leaf at a time into a saucer of clean water and gently rub the leaf tissue away from the skeleton. Be careful not to damage the veins of the leaf, because these are very delicate. If the tissue does not come away easily, put the leaf back in the jar for another week and then try again.

When all the tissue has been removed, the skeleton of the leaf will be left. Wash it several times in clean water and dry it between sheets of blotting paper.

Now you can paint the leaf, or simply mount it on a sheet of colored paper and frame it.

If you want the skeleton to be white, wash the leaf in a very weak solution of bleach. Don't leave it to soak too long or it will dissolve, and don't make the solution too strong or it will burn your fingers. Experiment with adding water to the bleach until you get it just right.

Screaming Skull

Have you ever wanted to see a screaming skull? You have? You've got to be out of your mind!

Well, this is your chance. Just look at the skull on this page for two or three minutes. Now look away from the book at a light-colored wall. You'll be able to see the skull, even though you aren't looking at it anymore. It's an optical illusion—or is it?

Harry the Hand

"Did you know there's a monster in the house?" you ask your friends.

They probably won't believe you. But you pick up a sandwich or an apple and say, "I'm going to feed him now."

Open the door to the room and stand in the doorway as you encourage your monster to come inside. While you pretend to talk to him, you are secretly putting a glove on your right hand. This glove has been covered with fuzzy material and it has false cardboard nails that you have glued onto the fingers to make it look like the hand of a horrible monster.

Now you start acting as if the monster is about to attack you. Say something like, "No—no! Horace! No—control yourself!" Since his name is Harry, this will drive him wild.

Suddenly, the monstrous hand grabs you by the throat, and you have quite a struggle getting out of his grip. As you can see from the illustration, the monster grabbing you is really your gloved hand.

AS SEEN THROUGH THE WALL

FURRY GLOVE ON YOUR OWN HAND

Your friends will watch in amazement as you go through your act. After a short struggle, you secretly remove the glove and order Harry back to his cage. Your audience should be really impressed with your bravery, but they have probably gotten fed up by now and are watching TV.

Shadow Ghost

This monster takes some preparation, but the effect is so ghostly that it is really worth the effort.

Get a large sheet of paper or cardboard and cut out the shapes of a pair of eyes, a nose and a horrible grinning mouth, like these shown in the first drawing.

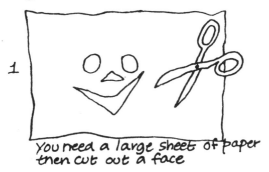

You need a large sheet of paper
then cut out a face

Tape the paper to a mirror. It is important that the paper is large enough to cover the whole mirror.

Tape the paper to
the mirror. It must cover
the whole mirror

At this point, ask one of your friends to help you with this "manifestation." Get your friend to stand facing the wall to one side of the mirror. Put the lights out. Now switch on a flashlight and hold it so your friend's shadow is reflected on the wall. It is also important that some of the light falls on the mirror.

You will probably have to get your friend to move a little, and you'll probably have to play a bit with the position of the flashlight and the mirror. But eventually you should be able to get the cut-out features from the mirror to be reflected in the correct place on the shadow of your friend.

When you finally get it right, there will be a very ghostly shadow on the wall. Call in the rest of your friends and family to see your ghastly ghostly visitor.

The Incredible Growing and Shrinking Ghost

Ghosts have a way of appearing only when it's dark. This one is no exception, because, when you put the lights out, a strange glow suddenly appears from nowhere.

Slowly the glow—a small circle of ghostly green

light—gets bigger and bigger. As it grows, it seems to transform itself into a glowing face. For a few minutes, the face is suspended in mid-air. Then it shrinks and finally disappears altogether. When the lights are switched back on, there is no clue to what could have caused this spooky phenomenon.

If any of your friends looked in your pocket, though, they would discover the very unspooky method you used to make this ghost materialize—an ordinary balloon! The face is drawn on the balloon with luminous paint. (You can get luminous paint in a hobby or modelling store.)

When the lights go out, you simply remove the balloon from your pocket and blow it up. When it is fully inflated, hold it for a few moments, then let the air out slowly, and replace it in your pocket.

The Incredible Growing and Shrinking Mobster

Put a huge overcoat over your shoulders and a hat on your head, and you are ready to show your friends this amazing illusion.

All you have to do is turn up the collar of the coat so that it touches the brim of your hat. Now turn your back on your friends.

Hold the hat and coat collar together in each hand. If you now lift your hands, it will look—from behind—as if you are growing in some weird way. Pull your hands down again—and you'll shrink.

It's important that no one sees your hands.

If you do it properly, this stunt is very convincing!

Being Bigfoot

Everyone has read about the large footprints supposedly left by the strange creature nicknamed Bigfoot. Maybe your parents have opinions about whether this creature really exists.

As you discuss it with them on a winter morning, you look out the window and gasp in amazement. There are gigantic tracks in the snow—footprints that could only be—you guessed it!

This should cause some consternation at your house. But actually, the footprints were made by you earlier in the day.

All you need are two buckets with handles and a stick—oh, yes, and most important, a snowfall! Put your feet into the buckets and hold on to the handles as you walk across the yard. Make your steps as wide as possible. Stop after each step and use the stick to make the marks of toes and claws in the snow.

Now you know how—all you have to do is wait for nature to cooperate.

2
SCREAMINGLY FUNNY

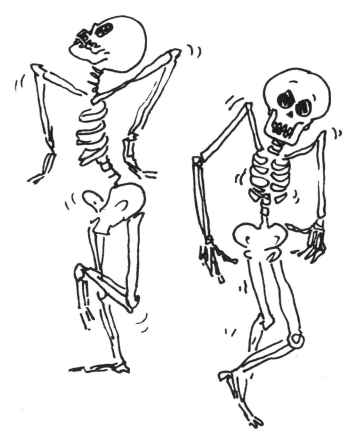

What is a ghost's favorite way to fly?
  On American Scarelines.

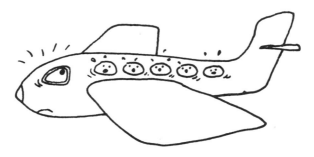

What is a ghost's favorite day of the week?
  Moanday.

What kind of ghost haunts Holiday Inns and arrests people?
  An inn-specter.

Why was the ghost arrested?
  He didn't have a haunting license.

If ghosts played soccer, who would stop the other team from scoring?
The ghoulie.

1ST GHOST: I saw *The Phantom of the Opera* last night.
2ND GHOST: Was it frightening?
1ST GHOST: Yes, it almost scared the life into me.

What jewels do ghosts wear?
Tombstones.

In what kind of plays do ghosts perform?
Phantom-imes.

What do ghosts eat for breakfast?
Dreaded Wheat.

What do ghouls eat for lunch?
Ghoulash.

What is a ghost's favorite dessert?
Boo-berry pie.

What does a ghost eat in an Italian restaurant?
Spook-getti.

What do ghouls call their navy?
The Ghost Guard.

Where do ghouls study?
At ghoul-lege (college).

What is the best way for ghost-hunters to keep fit?
They should exorcise regularly.

What is a ghost's favorite game?
Haunt and Seek.

What did one ghost say to the other ghost?
"Do you believe in people?"

Why are ghosts such bad liars?
You can see right through them.

What do ghosts like to sing?
Haunting melodies.

MOTHER GHOUL (to SON): "Only spook when you are spooken to."

Where do ghost trains appear?
At a manifestation.

How do ghosts pass through a locked door?
They use a skeleton key.

What do you call ghosts who live on the top floors of skyscrapers?
  High spirits.

What do you get if you cross a ghost, a potato, and a baseball fan?
  A spook-tater.

Where do ghosts go on vacation?
To the Dead Sea.

What sort of people sail on a ghost ship?
A skeleton crew.

What do near-sighted ghosts wear?
   Spook-tacles.

3
GHOSTLY TRICKS

The Ghost Walks

Imagine being able to hypnotize a friend so that he or she floats in the air like a ghost! Sounds impossible, doesn't it? But it is really simple. Here is how you accomplish this spooktacular illusion.

First you have to make a very special—and very secret—piece of equipment. You'll need two broom handles, two pieces of heavy cardboard and two tacks. Cut each piece of cardboard into a thin, oblong shape. Then use the tacks to attach them to one end of the broom handles.

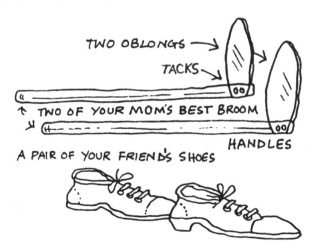

Hide the prepared broom handles behind a couch. Then, when you're ready to perform the trick, ask your friend—who must be in on the trick—to lie down behind the couch. As soon as he is out of sight, he removes his shoes and places them over the cardboard shapes. Then he kneels down and holds the end of each broom handle under his arms.

You'll also need a large sheet to perform this trick. Show the audience the sheet and use it to cover your friend behind the couch. As you let go of the sheet, he stands up. The sheet falls over his neck, covering the broom handles up to the shoes. It should look as if the sheet is covering your friend from his neck to his feet.

Then he walks around the room—and it looks as if he is floating in the air!

At this point, if you want, you can "accidentally" stand on one edge of the sheet, so it pulls off and reveals how the trick is done.

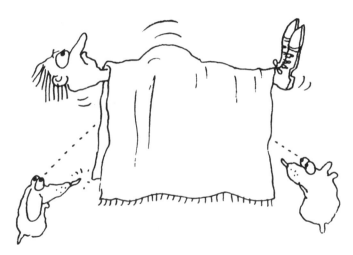

Ghost in Your Pocket

"Have you ever seen a ghost?" you ask your friends. Most of them will admit that they haven't. You then boast that not only have you seen a ghost, but you have a tame one in your pocket.

You then prove your claim by removing a matchbox from your pocket. Placing the box on the back of your hand, you tell everyone that the ghost is inside the box because he (or maybe it's a she—it's sometimes hard to tell with ghosts) prefers to stay in the dark.

You can, however, prove that the ghost really exists by asking it to open the matchbox. Much to your friends' amazement, the box begins to creep across your hand of its own accord! Then it stands up—creepier and creepier! And then it slowly opens! It must be a ghost: What other explanation can there be?

Well, there is of course another explanation. And it is a really simple one—trickery. The matchbox is not moved or opened by ghostly means, but by a piece of thread.

When the drawer is pushed in, the thread is pushed down to the end of the sleeve (Pulling the thread will make the drawer rise.)

knot

To create this ghostly phenomenon, you have to attach the thread to the matchbox as shown in the diagram. To do this, you need to thread a needle, remove the drawer from the matchbox, and push the needle through the outer part of the box from front to back (or back to front, we don't care).

Leave a small length of thread loose at the front of the matchbox and hold it in position with some sticky tape. So that your friends don't see this secret preparation, glue a label from another matchbox into place on top of the first label.

Slip the drawer back into the outside of the matchbox and your preparation is almost complete.

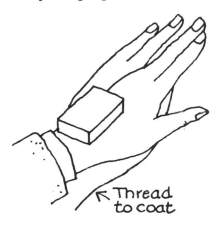

All you have to do now is to tie the end of the thread to your belt or to a buttonhole. The length of the thread you need depends on the length of your arm. It should be just long enough so that you can place the matchbox on your hand without any problem—but short enough so that it is stretched all the way when you move your hand forward slightly. After a few experiments, you will probably get it right. Place the matchbox in a convenient pocket until you are ready to do the trick.

Then take the box from your pocket and place it on the back of your hand. Position the thread so that it runs through your fingers (as in the illustration).

Move your hand slightly and, as the thread tightens, the box will move. Move your hand forward and the box will suddenly stand on end. Keep moving your hand forward and the box will open mysteriously!

If your friends ask why they cannot see the tame ghost, tell them he is only visible at night. Or that he only shows himself to friends. Or his ectoplasm isn't strong enough.

If someone gets suspicious and wants to examine the matchbox, pretend that the ghost has escaped. Quickly slip the box into your pocket and frantically search around on the floor, or in other rooms, for the slippery spirit.

Eventually you "find" the ghost (you need to be a pretty good actor for this) and you take the matchbox from your pocket and pop him into it. The matchbox you take from your pocket, though, is not the same matchbox you used before—but one that looks just the same—and that you had in your pocket all the time.

Your friends can examine it for as long as they like, provided they don't let the ghost escape again—for the trick matchbox stays hidden away in your pocket.

Allow your friends to examine the matchbox

Mystery of the Skulls

Draw four small skulls on a sheet of paper, as shown in the illustration. Now turn the paper over and you are ready to demonstrate the mystery of the skulls. The dotted lines show the position of the skulls that are drawn on the other side of the page, but your friends are not aware of their existence.

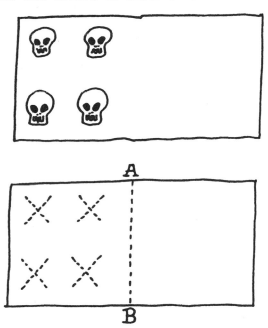

Tear the paper in half from A to B. Casually turn over the right half and place it beneath the left half. Turn over both pieces of paper and then tear them in half once again.

Now place one set of papers on top of the other (it doesn't matter which way). Now turn the papers over and tear them in half once more.

Once again place either set of papers on top of the other.

You now hold eight pieces of paper.

So far no one will realize that every alternate piece of paper has a skull drawn on the bottom of it—because the way you handled the paper kept the skulls hidden at all times.

Deal the pieces into two piles with the first piece going to the left, the second to the right the third to the left and so on.

Ask a friend to touch one of the piles. If he touches the left-hand pile, ask him to hold it in his fist.

Show the papers in the right-hand pile and draw a skull on each one.

Then have your friend open his fist. A skull will have "mysteriously" appeared on each one of the papers he holds.

If your friend should choose the right-hand pile, do exactly the same thing. Draw a skull on each of the pieces in the right-hand pile and then ask your friend to turn over the pieces on the table. Each one bears a skull!

It must be skullduggery. . . .

Hunt the Skeleton

If your friends would like to be ghost-hunters, you can get them to try this test. Show them three haunted houses—actually, three matchboxes—and tell them that one is haunted by a skeleton. To prove it, you pick up one of the haunted houses and shake it. Your friends will hear the ghostly rattling of the skeleton's bones inside the box. Then you shake the other two boxes, but all they hear is a ghostly silence.

Now you shuffle the boxes around on the table, and your friends have to guess which haunted house contains the skeleton. But they fail every time. No matter how carefully they watch you mix the boxes, they will never find anything inside the matchbox.

What your friends don't know is that none of the boxes contains anything at all. You have a fourth box, containing some pebbles or old matchsticks (or bones, if you have some), tied to your right arm with a strip of adhesive tape. Your coat sleeve hides this secret box from view.

When you use your right hand to shake one of the three boxes on the table, it seems as if the sound is coming from that box. But the rattling noise actually is coming from the concealed box. When you use your left hand to shake a box, nothing is heard.

In this way, you can make the rattling sounds come from any box you choose, and convince your friends that they will never be any good as ghost-hunters.

Never tell them how you cheated. Keep the secret up your sleeve. . . .

Ghostly Symbols

You tell a friend that you can get in touch with ghosts. To prove your claim, you show a sheet of stiff cardboard. It is obvious to your friend that there is absolutely nothing written on either side of the cardboard.

Next, ask your friend to hold the cardboard on her head while you summon up the spirits. To do this, you can mutter some magic words, stomp around the room or do anything strange or mysterious. When your friend removes the cardboard from her head, it is covered with mystical symbols (the card, not the head).

How is it done? Simple. You make use of another friend who is in on the trick—an unseen friend. You also need two pieces of cardboard, both the same shape and size. One is completely blank on both

sides and the other is covered with stars, crescent moons and other mystical symbols (here are some shapes you can copy).

Before your victim arrives on the scene, get your accomplice to hide behind the curtains with the card bearing the mystical symbols. Place a chair in front of the curtains and you're ready for your victim.

When she arrives, get her to sit on the chair by the curtains. Show her the blank cardboard. Make sure she's convinced that the cardboard is blank before you go any further. Then bring the cardboard up above the victim's head as you say, "Will you just hold this on your head for a moment?"

As soon as the card is well above your victim's head, you hand it to your friend behind the curtain, who exchanges it for the cardboard with the writing on it. Place the "mystical" cardboard on your victim's head and get her to hold it there with both hands. You have thus exchanged the cards without your victim realizing that anything unusual has happened.

Now go through your mumbo-jumbo routine as if you're getting in touch with the ghost world. When your victim removes the card from her head, she will have no idea whatsoever how the magic signs appeared on it!

4
MONSTER PRANKS & PRACTICAL JOKES

Message from the Spirits

To most people this message looks like just a bunch of unrelated scribbles, but you and your friends can read it easily.

First fold a sheet of paper into three unequal sections, as shown in the picture. Then write a message across the folds, as shown in the second picture.

When you open the paper, it is practically impossible to read the message. To make it even more mysterious, you can dress it up with mystical signs (see page 43 for ideas).

If the message was really from the spirits, it would probably have been written in blood. But since it's not, a red pen will do. You can always say it's dragon's blood.

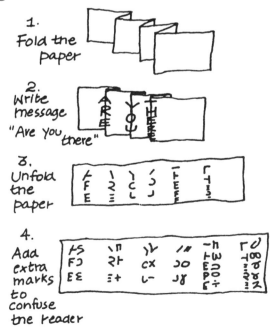

1. Fold the paper

2. Write message "Are you there"

3. Unfold the paper

4. Add extra marks to confuse the reader

Ghost in a Glass

Tie one end of a piece of string around a glass and the other end around a pencil. Make sure to tie the string securely or you might end up breaking the glass.

Half fill the glass with water and you are ready to demonstrate the power of the spirit world. Hold the pencil in your hand and let the half-filled glass hang freely. Tell everyone that this strange contraption is like a radio, but it only receives messages from ghosts.

Suddenly there is a distinct tap, then another, then more. They seem to be coming from the glass, but there is no logical explanation for them. Your friends must be convinced that you are receiving messages from ghosts.

But the explanation is much simpler than that. To produce the taps, all you have to do is twist the pencil. When you do this, the string slips a little to produce the mysterious sounds.

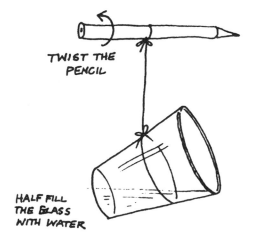

TWIST THE
PENCIL

HALF FILL
THE GLASS
WITH WATER

Get the Ghost in the Picture

Over the years, many ghost-hunters have tried to photograph ghosts. Some photos have been published that seem to show ghosts, but in most cases they have been exposed as deliberate fakes. It's not difficult to fake a ghost photo. Here's how you do it:

Take a photograph of a friend standing in front of your house. Get him or her to move out of the way quickly and then take a second photograph on the same frame of film. With a bit of luck, you will end up with a ghost image of your friend on the finished photograph.

If your camera doesn't allow you to take more than one picture on a frame, wind the film on but with the rewind button pressed down. This disengages the ratchet that holds the film so it won't wind forward. In this way you can get two exposures on the same frame. (It is not possible to do this with films that are inside a cassette.)

When taking ghost pictures like this, mount your camera on a tripod, if you can get one, so that it doesn't move from one picture to the next.

The Headless Ghost

Here is another ghost picture you can try. Set your camera to a slow exposure and get someone to stand in front of it. During the exposure, get him to nod his head up and down. With a bit of luck (like most ghost pictures, this doesn't always work perfectly), you will get a picture of your friend without a head!

You always suspected that he didn't have much upstairs, didn't you? Now you can prove it!

Ghost Writing

Ever heard of a ghost that writes? No, not a ghost-writer! This is writing that appears on a slate when you hold it up in a darkened room and ask the spirits for a message.

Luminous paint—mixed with a small piece of beeswax—is all that these particular spirits are made of. You can get luminous paint in a hobby or modelling shop. By mixing the paint and the beeswax together, you can make a crayon that writes with a glow.

All you have to do is switch off the lights, bring out a blackboard and remove the luminous beeswax crayon from your pocket. Write on the slate and the glowing writing seems to appear by itself.

What do you write on the slate? Well, that's up to you, but try to make it funny if you can.

HANDS UP, THE GHOST THAT CAN WRITE.

The Clammy Thing

"There are ghosts and monsters all around us, They can materialize at any time and in any place. You know, there could even be weird things in this room right now," you say to a friend while he's putting his coat on.

Keep talking like this and try to convince your friend that he could come across something supernatural at any time. Sooner or later he will put his hand into his pocket. When he does, it will come into contact with a strange, wobbly, cold and clammy thing that is enough to make his flesh crawl.

If your friend is fairly level-headed, get out of the way quickly, because it won't be long before he takes that clammy thing out of his pocket. When he does, he will realize that you planted it there, because it is a balloon filled with water!

The Invisible Man

You have the power to make people become invisible. "I don't believe that," says one of your friends. "What!" you exclaim. "Are you calling me a liar? Of course I can. And what's more, I can prove it."

At this point you take your friend outside and explain that you can make him invisible and will do it right now. You make some mystical signs around him and mutter a spell. Any spell will do, but if you don't know any, you can use the one below:

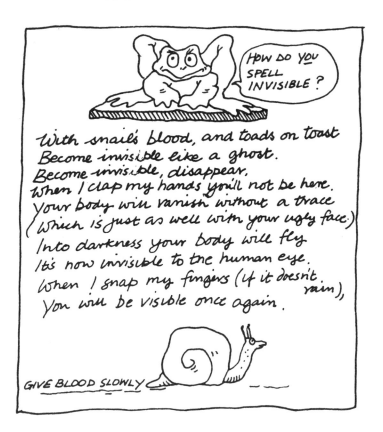

HOW DO YOU SPELL INVISIBLE?

With snail's blood, and toads on toast
Become invisible like a ghost.
Become invisible, disappear,
When I clap my hands you'll not be here.
Your body will vanish without a trace
(Which is just as well with your ugly face.)
Into darkness your body will fly
It's now invisible to the human eye.
When I snap my fingers (if it doesn't rain),
You will be visible once again.

GIVE BLOOD SLOWLY

When you're finished, act as if you can't see him. Ask him to go back into the next room with you. When you get there, no one else can see your friend either. Some ask where he went. Others make wisecracks about him. From their actions and remarks, it is obvious that he is completely invisible.

You now snap your fingers and your friend becomes visible again. Everyone gasps with amazement at his sudden re-appearance.

"Hello, Charlie," they say. "Where have you been?" Which will be really surprising to him if his name is not Charlie. But whatever his name is, he may now wonder if you really can make people invisible. With a bit of luck he won't ask you to do it again!

Touch of Evil

When you start talking about ghosts, there is always someone who refuses to believe in them. Here is one way to prove that there are mysterious forces all around us.

Ask everyone except your victim to leave the room—or at least stand a long distance away—so your victim doesn't think anyone is helping you.

Tell him to face you as you point both your index fingers towards his eyes. You inform him that holding your two fingers in this position is a sign of evil and that you are going to summon up dark forces to prove to him that invisible powers do exist.

Move your hands towards your victim's head. Just before your fingers touch them, get him to close his eyes. In a quiet and mysterious voice, ask him if he can sense the presence of invisible spirits in the room.

He'll say no, but just as he does, a ghost taps him on the back of his head. Naturally, he opens his eyes immediately as you move your fingers away from them. He may then look around to see who tapped

him—but no one is there. It must have been a
spirit!

The "spirit" is created by the clever way that you
touch your victim's eyelids. You bring your fingers
towards his eyes as described before. But as soon as
his eyes close, you spread the middle and index
fingers of your right hand and touch his eyelids with
them. This leaves your left hand free to tap him on
the back of his head.

skeptic

Immediately bring your left hand, with index
finger extended, back to its original position in front
of his face and slowly withdraw your pointing
fingers away as he opens his eyes. He will believe
that both hands were touching him and, since there
is no one else who could have tapped him, he may
begin to believe in ghosts after all!

The Poltergeist Effect

The lights are out; the atmosphere is creepy; there is an unearthly stillness . . . Aaagh, what was that? An eerie light flashed across the room. There's another—and another—*aaagh!*

Any spooky evening is bound to be a screaming success when these mysterious balls of light start darting around the room.

They are extremely ghostly—but they are nothing more than Ping-Pong balls covered with luminous paint. When the lights are out, start throwing them around the room.

At first they may give your friends a bit of a scare, but sooner or later someone will pick one up from the floor and throw it back across the room. Before long everyone else will be doing the same thing—and the room will be full of flying lights. This is a great icebreaker for parties.

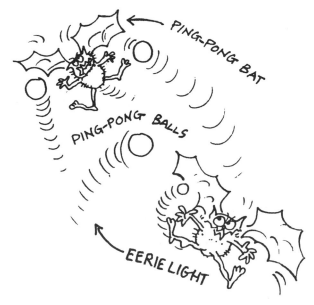

5
HAUNTING YOUR OWN HOUSE

Strange Noises

Imagine talking to your friends about ghosts and monsters and dark corners—and suddenly hearing ghastly groans, clanking chains, creaking doors and the wailing of banshees! And all this in your own house! It's enough to make you want to leave home!

If you have really set the right atmosphere with your stories and talk of ghosts, these noises will get your friends pretty nervous. And yet all you need to produce them is a tape recorder—and some trickiness.

The secret is that only half the tape has anything recorded on it. This is how you do it:

Put a fresh tape into your recorder. Run it forward—without recording anything—until you are halfway through the tape. Now start making as many ghostly noises as you can. (You'll find some ideas for this on pages 60–63.)

Rewind the tape and you're ready. When your friends arrive, switch the tape on. It will be running while you're talking to them, but because there is nothing on the first half no one will realize that the tape recorder is switched on. That's the reason for leaving the first half of the tape blank. It would look very suspicious if you switched the machine on only seconds before the noises started. This way, no one will suspect that a tape recorder is being used.

Another way you can use the tape is to switch it on just before you go out for the evening. The people left in the house will get quite a shock when they hear horrible sounds sometime later. When you get back, you will probably find that their hair has turned white with shock. (This does not apply to bald people.)

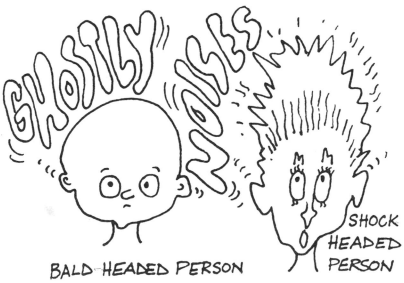

BALD-HEADED PERSON

SHOCK HEADED PERSON

Getting Ghastly Sounds on Tape

It is amazing what frighteningly realistic ghostly sound effects you can record on tape with just a little thought and ingenuity. Here are a few things you can try, but see if you can come up with sound inventions of your own as well.

Ominous thunder: Shake a tin tray between your hands.

Clanking chains: Rattle a few small empty cans.

Creaking door: If you have one in your house, make a recording of it. It will sound really eerie when you play it back loudly late at night.

Howling hounds: If your dog ever howls, get your tape recorder to him quickly. Provided that he doesn't get self-conscious, you could end up with what sounds like *The Hound of the Baskervilles.*

Rattling bones: Hold three or four pencils loosely in your hand and then shake your hand so the pencils knock together.

Ghoulish screams: Scream into a jelly jar (take the jelly out first)—it sounds really strange when played back.

Howling wind: Blow across the top of an empty bottle.

Ghostly footsteps: Simply tap on a table.

Terrifying sounds: Wail, groan, howl and scream.

One tip: It's a good idea to do your recording in the bathroom or in an empty (preferably haunted) room. The echo you get greatly adds to the effectiveness of the result.

Nuts!

Here is another sound you can make for your ghostly recording—the noise of horses' hooves pulling a phantom coach.

You need two coconuts. At the top of each coconut you will find three soft spots. Make holes at these points and pour out the milk from inside. This is really good to drink. Next, eat out the contents of the coconuts (that's the best part of this trick!) and then start knocking the shells together. Instant clattering hooves!

One more thing about those soft spots at the top of the coconut. You may think that they were put there just so that you could get the milk out. But you are absolutely wrong! The holes you make in these soft spots are specially needed so that you can put string through them and make handles for your clattering hoof sound-makers. (Isn't it marvelous what fascinating facts you can learn reading an educational book like this one!)

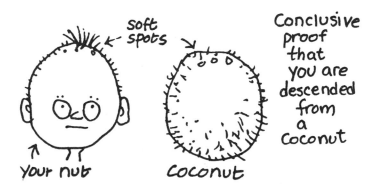

soft spots

Conclusive proof that you are descended from a coconut

your nut

coconut

Footsteps of Dracula

In the middle of the night, there is an eerie tapping noise coming from the kitchen. Is it a poltergeist, the footsteps of Dracula—or the dripping of blood onto a stone slab? Only you know the answer, and you are in bed (laughing your head off).

What is that horrible sound that is scaring everyone out of their skin? It's dried peas. What? Yes, dried peas are the cause of the ghostly noises—helped along by a little secret work of yours just before you went to bed.

Just before bedtime you crept into the kitchen and balanced a tin tray on top of a glass. Then you put a wine glass on the tray and filled it to overflowing with dried peas. Now you put a little water in the glass and went to bed. (If you put too much water in, the peas would just get soggy and you'd end up with pea soup.)

After a while the water soaked into the peas and made them swell. When this happened there wasn't enough room for all of them in the wine glass, so they fell out onto the tray, making a noise as they landed.

It could be a ghost; it could be a horrible beast—it could be a werewolf tapping on the window. One thing it just cannot be is you—for you are tucked away for the night.

6
MONSTER LAUGHS

What do you say to a three-headed ghoul?
  "Hello, hello, hello."

Why did the ghoul go to the hospital?
  To have its ghoul-stones removed.

How does a monster count to 23?
   On its fingers.

Why are monster's fingers never more than eleven
inches long?
   *Because if they were twelve inches they'd be a
   foot.*

Why are monsters forgetful?
   *Because everything you tell them goes in one ear
   and out the other.*

What do you do with a green monster?
  Wait until it ripens.

What do you call a handsome, friendly, likeable monster?
  A failure.

Where do monsters travel?
  From ghost to ghost.

MOTHER MONSTER (*to* BABY MONSTER): "Don't eat chicken with your fingers. Eat your fingers separately."

What does a monster call its parents?
Deady and Mummy.

MY DEADY AND MY MUMMY

Where do you find giant snails?
   At the end of giants' fingers.

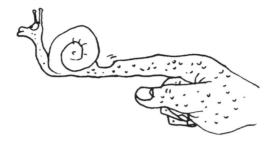

What do monsters like on their roast beef?
   Grave-y.

What does a monster do when it loses a hand?
   It goes to a second-hand shop.

Which is the unluckiest monster?
   The Luck Less Monster (the Loch Ness monster).

What type of ices do monsters like?
I-screams for help.

How does a witch tell time?
With a witch-watch.

What goes ha, ha, ha, bonk?
A monster laughing its head off.

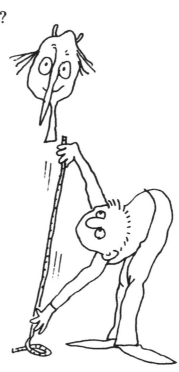

What's the best way to talk to a monster?
Long distance.

Why are banshees always female?
  Because if they were male, they would be ban-hes.

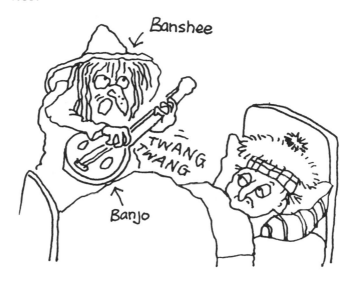

What scary creature is gray, eats peanuts and is a little crazy?
  An ele-mental.

What happened when the boy monster met the girl monster?

It was love at first fright.

Who won the monster beauty contest?

No one.

What does a monster do when it loses a tail?

It goes to a retailer.

What do monsters do at eleven o'clock in the morning?

Take a coffin break.

What trees do monsters like best?
  Ceme-trees (cemeteries).

What is a monster's favorite fruit dessert?
  Leeches and scream (peaches and cream).

"Mommy, mommy, all my friends say I look like a monster!"
  "Don't worry about it, dear. Now go and comb your face."

The Monster's Finger

Tell your friends that on your last trip to Outer Mongolia you came across an enormous, ferocious monster. Unfortunately, you couldn't capture it, but as it ran to escape from you, it lost one of its fingers and—surprise, surprise—you managed to recover it and bring it home for all your friends to see.

You remove a matchbox from your pocket, open it up and there, resting in the drawer—is a gruesome, severed finger. *Aaaagh!*

But the finger is not, of course, really from a monster. It is really yours! This is how you do it:

First you must prepare the matchbox by cutting a small hole in the bottom of the drawer. This hole must be large enough for you to put your finger through.

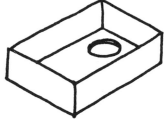

In the bottom of the matchbox cover, cut a slot just a little wider than the width of your finger.

For added realism, smear some lipstick and perhaps

some mascara on your finger to make it look bloody and bruised. A little bit of "blood-stained" (amazing what red ink will do!) cotton in the drawer will hide the hole.

With the matchbox ready in your pocket, you can start your incredible story. Remove the box from your pocket, secretly insert your finger through the hole, and (thanks to the slot in the bottom) open the box to show the monster's finger inside.

If you're a good story-teller, some of your friends may actually believe that you are showing them the severed finger of a Mongolian monster.

As a frightening finish to your tale, you could say there is a legend that if a piece of the monster's body breaks off, it will grow into a new monster.

"But I don't believe this story," you tell your friends. "I don't see how it's possible for. . . . aaagh!"

At this point, you wiggle your finger, all your friends faint, and you close the box as fast as you can.

Skull of Mystery

Cut the shape of a skull out of cardboard. Cut out holes for the eyes and the mouth. Nail the cardboard skull to a piece of wood as in the illustration. Then paint the wood and the back of the skull with flat black paint.

Paint the face of the skull with luminous paint. This is quite expensive, so don't make your skull too large. (You can buy luminous paint in a hobby shop or modelling store.)

Leave the skull in the light all day, for it is the reaction of the paint to light that makes it glow in the dark.

Just before your victim arrives at your house—or wherever the mysterious skull is going to materialize—hide the cardboard skull under a cushion or somewhere else where it cannot be seen, but where you can get at it easily.

When the time is right, turn out the lights, quickly put on a black glove, which you also have handy, and take the skull out from its hiding place.

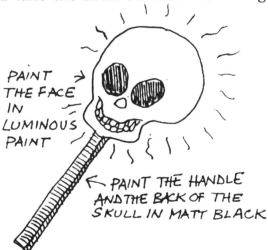

PAINT THE FACE IN LUMINOUS PAINT

PAINT THE HANDLE AND THE BACK OF THE SKULL IN MATT BLACK

Keep the painted side of the cardboard towards you at first and then turn it around so that it faces your friends. They will jump out of their skin as the grinning skull appears in the darkness!

Wave it around a few times, groan a little, and then turn the painted side back towards you—to make it disappear. Do it slowly this time, and the skull will seem to fade away into nothing.

Hide the skull and the glove away and then switch the lights on. Your friends may also have disappeared. (They'll be behind the couch.)

Another way to use the skull is to do away with the wooden handle. Instead, attach the skull to some black thread. hang the thread over a light fixture or some other object that's high up. By pulling on the thread, you can make the skull float in the air in a very eerie way. Don't forget to put the lights out first!

Mystical Music

You show your friends a tambourine and place it on the table. Then you hold a large handkerchief up in front of it. Both your hands are visible and yet, through some unseen force, the handkerchief begins to shake and the tambourine rattles. As it is obvious that no one else is around to help, this weird activity must be a supernatural phenomenon, right?

Wrong. The only super force around is a piece of thread. This is tied from the top left corner of the handkerchief to the top right corner. You will also need a small hook screwed into the wood around the side of the tambourine.

After you place the tambourine on the table and hold the handkerchief in front of it, bring your hands together. The thread will slacken. Then try to hook the thread onto the hook on the tambourine.

As soon as the thread catches on the hook, pull your hands apart and then back together several times. This tightens and loosens the thread, pulling the tambourine up and down sharply. This causes it to make sounds that your audience will think is created by restless spirits. Little do they know *how* restless!

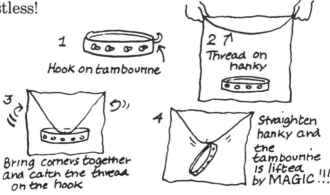

1   Hook on tambourine

2   Thread on hanky

3   Bring corners together and catch the thread on the hook

4   Straighten hanky and the tambourine is lifted by MAGIC!!!

Unearthly Shrieks in the Night

The next time you have a friend (it might happen!)
stay over, tell him a scary ghost story before he goes
to bed. If you also do some of the spooky stunts from
this book, he will be a basket case by bedtime.

As he walks into the bedroom, he hears a ghostly
wail. Don't stand too near him for he is likely to
jump out of his skin.

But there is nothing at all for him to be worried
about. What he thinks is a ghostly wail is simply an
ordinary violin that you rigged up in a special way.

Before your friend arrives, put a violin on a table
in the bedroom. (If you can't find a violin, don't try
doing this with a grand piano—it doesn't work.)
Attach a weight to a long cord, place the cord over
the strings of the violin and then tie the other end
to the door handle.

When your victim walks into the room, the weight
pulls the cord over the violin strings. This makes a
really unearthly sound. You could explain this to
your friend afterwards, but by that time he is likely
to be many miles away.

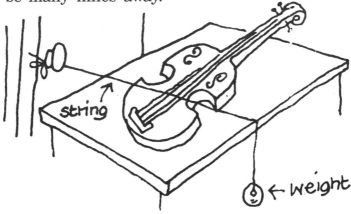

Floating Spirits

Here is another trick for terrifying someone who is going to bed. All you need is a sheet of paper, a long piece of thread and some sticky tape.

Use the tape to attach one end of the thread to the paper. Place the paper on top of a tall piece of furniture in your victim's bedroom. Now run the thread across the room, under the door and to your bedroom—or wherever you decide to hide.

When your victim goes to bed, wait for a while (just long enough to give him time to get into bed and doze off). As soon as you think the time is right, start making some ghostly noises and mysterious bumps in the night.

After a while your victim should be awake enough for you to "send in" the ghost. Give a quick tug on your end of the thread. This will pull the paper off the tall piece of furniture and it will float gently down to the floor. Your victim will not see it as a gently wafting, harmless sheet of paper, but as a creepy piece of ectoplasm with scary intentions.

If you want, you can place more than one of these floating spirits in your victim's room, but watch out that you don't get your threads tangled.

Window Tapper

You may want to try another diabolical bedroom trick. Tie a piece of thread to the center of a short stick. Tie the other end to a window fastening in the bedroom of your intended victim.

Open the window and hang the stick outside. Close the window and draw the curtains.

During the night, especially if it is a windy one, the stick will tap against the window in a very spooky way. It should give whoever is sleeping in that room quite a scare.

Creepy Crawlies

Buy a package of pipe cleaners and you are ready to make creepy-crawly creatures that will make people frantic.

Cut a pipe cleaner into inch-long lengths. Dip

these short pieces into green dye—or color them with a green felt-tipped pen. These little bits of pipe cleaner make fairly realistic-looking caterpillars. You can leave them in a friend's shoe, a bed, or if you really want to set your family against you— in a salad. Do it after everyone has finished eating!

If you cut a few pipe cleaners into two-inch lengths, and then twist four of these lengths together, you will produce some horrible spiders. For a terrifying effect, you can paint or dye them gray or black.

Like the caterpillars, these spiders can be left around the house in interesting places to scare the wits out of anyone who comes across them. You can also try hanging a spider from a lampshade, a picture or some other object.

A very effective trick is to attach one of these spiders to a thread and hang it over a high object. If you hold the other end of the thread, you can make the spider go up and down—much to the horror of the poor unfortunate onlooker.

8
TERRIBLE
TRIVIA

Is Friday the 13th really unlucky?

They think so in France. Search through the whole country and you won't find a house that bears the number 13—there is no such thing. Nor is there a room 13 in any French hotel.

In Paris it is possible to hire people called *quatorziemes* (fourteenths) to come to your dinner party so that you won't have to have 13 people around the table.

In England it was once believed that couples who kissed 13 times on one day would soon part.

No bones about it: It was once believed that you shouldn't give your dog a bone 13 days before Midsummer's Day or 13 days after (Midsummer's Day is June 24th, so that would be on June 11th or on July 5th). If you did, people said he'd go mad and attack you.

Never give a dog a bone thirteen days before or after MIDSUMMER'S DAY

According to superstition, Friday is a bad day for everybody. For example, all these things happened on Fridays:

> Adam and Eve ate the apple.
> Adam and Eve died.
> Cain slew Abel.
> The great flood started.
> Jesus Christ was crucified.

Superstitious sailors won't leave port on a Friday. At one time this idea was so prevalent that the British Admiralty tried to get rid of it by laying the keel of a new ship on a Friday. They called the ship Friday. Captain Friday was given command. The ship was launched on a Friday. It went out to sea and was never seen again!

If you cut your fingernails on a Friday, people used to believe you'd bring unhappiness upon yourself. And the same thing would happen if you burned any letters on that fateful day.

But Friday doesn't have to be all bad. If you dream on a Friday, and tell someone about it the next day, then that dream will come true.

So is Friday the 13th doubly unlucky? If you think so, maybe you'd like to try some of the things that are supposed to bring good luck.

Catch a falling leaf.

Touch wood.

Find a four-leaf clover.

Cross your fingers.

Hang a horseshoe in the house.

Find a frog.

If all else fails, you can always use the sure-fire bringer of good luck—put your clothes on inside out!

Can you really predict the future by throwing dice?

Some people think so. It may not be scientific—but it's fun. Here's how you do it:

Put three dice in a cup and then cast with your left hand into a circle you draw on a piece of paper on the table. These are the predictions for the total of the numbers you throw:

    3. A pleasant surprise.
    4. An unpleasant happening.
    5. A new friend.
    6. The loss of something you value.
    7. People will say mean things about you.
    8. Your sins will find you out.

    9. Romance is in the air.
  10. A birth in the family.
  11. Someone you know
       will get sick.

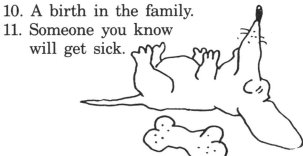

12. News through the mail.

13. Something will upset you.
14. A new admirer.

15. Good luck and happiness.
16. Money and good luck.
17. A pleasant journey.
18. Something really special will happen.

9
FANG-TASTIC!

I'm the eeriest

Who has feathers, fangs and goes quack?
Count Duckula.

How do you join Dracula's fan club?
Send in your name, address and blood type.

Who did Dracula marry?
The ghoul necks door.

What should you do if you receive a present from Dracula?
Send him a fang-you note.

How does Dracula start a letter?
Tomb it may concern.

What kind of boats do vampires like?
Blood vessels.

What kind of vans do vampires like to drive?
Bloodmobiles.

Why do vampires brush their teeth in the morning?
To stop bat breath.

What did the vampire say to his dentist after he got his new false teeth?
"Fangs very much."

What do vampires take for a bad cold?
Coffin medicine.

What is Dracula's favorite song?
"Fangs for the Memory."

Why was Dracula unhappy in love?
He loved in vein.

What is Dracula's favorite dance?
The fang-dango.

Where does Dracula keep his money?
In a blood bank.

What Dracula ask the blood bank?
"Do you deliver?"

Why is it so easy to fool a vampire?
Because they are all suckers.

Why should vampires be locked up?
Because they're all bats.

Where does Dracula get his jokes?
From his crypt writer.

INDEX